3

by Kathy Joyce

Cover illustration: Alex Eben Meyer
Book design: Joe Lops

Addington CF and LTC Bodoni typefaces
provided by The Type Founders
thetypefounders.com

979-8-9918334-4-8

For Ivy

CONTENTS

BASEBALL

ON JUNE 8TH, 2025, I WENT TO MY FIRST baseball game at Yankee Stadium.

The New York Yankees were playing against the Boston Red Sox.

It was one of the most interesting things I have ever witnessed.

I was stunned and shocked.

I Was Stunned and Shocked at the Baseball Game

My first shocking observation was that everyone at Yankee Stadium is a jock and a prep. A lot of people have blonde hair and sunburns or suntans. No one there is gothic; however some people are Latino. The only person who was even a little bit gothic was the man who checked my bag. He was really cool. He kept saying, "It doesn't even matter. Doesn't matter."

My second shocking observation was how many people were there, probably about ten thousand, and I did not fit in with any of them. I did not fit in and I felt like a freak, especially around the Red Sox fans who were extremely menacing and evil.

My third shocking observation was that all of the Yankees fans were wearing the exact same jersey. The Aaron Judge jersey with the 99 on the back. I understand that he is the best player on the team, and I also understand that he is handsome. However, I believed in the baseball world of my mind, in which everyone picks a favorite player aside from Aaron Judge and they purchase a jersey for said player to show support for him.

This makes sense to me because it seems like Aaron Judge is already very famous and reaping the spiritual rewards from all the fans who wear his jersey, so we should send some of our psychic energy to a less famous player. This is sort of how I chose my favorite player, Anthony Volpe.

How it Started With Anthony Volpe

When I first started watching baseball, I noticed that Anthony Volpe had the number 11 on his back, which is my favorite number and my lucky number. So I decided to become interested in him. It turned out that he was Filipino and just had something about him like a twinkle in his eye and there was just something very charming about him. And he was doing very well at the last World Series, which made me feel less pathetic and worthless. That's the thing about baseball. It goes both ways.

The Highs and Lows of Baseball

When the Yankees lose I become suicidal. It's extremely upsetting to me. I hate the other teams too. In the beginning I was fascinated with baseball as a whole and I was relatively happy for all of the players. I really loved Shohei Ohtani. Now when I see the Dodgers I just scream. And I hate it the most when anyone that's not on the Yankees hits a home run.

But when the Yankees win a game it feels so good. Sometimes it makes me cry. It feels like there is magic in the air and anything is possible. The connection between the fans and the team is strong and beautiful. I love to see the players celebrating and smiling. There's things you can do to help your team win, which is a really incredible experience that I experienced at Yankee Stadium. Cheering for a player can make them more confident which can make them hit the ball.

There are other things that I can do to help my team win, like eating bananas.

How Bananas Relate to Baseball

The thing with the bananas started after the last World Series. Since the Yankees lost and I hated bananas, I decided to purchase one and eat it as a form of self-harm. Because I hated myself and my life. However, I actually kind of enjoyed the banana and I started to eat bananas regularly. This ended up being very positive for my life because it turned out I had a severe potassium deficiency which doctors were very worried about. So every time the Yankees would play a game I would eat two bananas. I would eat the bananas and the Yankees would play and the Yankees would win.

It became clear that the bananas were causing them to win. To see if it was a coincidence, I did not eat the bananas last week, and the Yankees were subsequently destroyed by the Dodgers. I laid on the floor and cried. You get a bad feeling when the Yankees lose. Like only bad things are going to keep happening all night. And they did.

I ate two bananas before I went to Yankee Stadium and they still lost, but it was not a humiliating loss. The point is I learned my lesson and you should eat two bananas when the Yankees are playing baseball. Alternatively, you can eat one banana and your friend or lover can eat one banana, but it's important that you eat the bananas together.

Now I Want to Talk About Anthony Volpe Again

When I sat in my seat at Yankee Stadium, I could see Anthony Volpe on the field. Right there, like it was no big deal. But it was a big deal to me and I could feel sensations in my heart. I actually used my heart to shoot beams of love towards each individual member of the Yankees when they were hitting the ball. I also shot beams of hatred towards each individual member of the Red Sox. I had to be careful when shifting between beams so that I did not accidentally shoot hatred towards the Yankees, but I messed up one time which is probably why they lost.

I kept thinking that if I really wanted to I could just jump onto the field and say "hello" to Anthony Volpe or to any of the other players for that matter. I mean I have so much to say to them. None of the other fans seemed to be freaking out about this. In fact, most of them were on their phones or talking to each other for the majority of the game. It was confusing to me that they would not stare at the game the entire time. They would clap and cheer when the Yankees were doing good, but they seemed to harbor a lot less resentment towards the other team than I did. I did not notice anyone other than myself screaming "NO!!!" when the Red Sox hit the ball, and I felt a bit self-conscious about it. But I could not stop myself. It's like when I transferred from Catholic school to public school, and I was accustomed to saying the pledge of allegiance along with all the prayers that we said in the morning, meaning we followed it all up with an "Amen." So when we finished saying the pledge on my first day of public school, I was the only one who said "Amen" and it was very embarrassing.

It's Extremely Interesting to Me to Look at the Behaviors of Baseball Players

I really like it when they tap their bats against the plate. I like all of the behaviors that the players do. Some of them lick their fingers for a moment, some of them chew on seeds, some of them touch their helmets. It seems like they are all doing things to give themselves luck, the same way that I eat the bananas. During a baseball game, an extremely high amount of "magic" and "luck" is happening in one place at one time. The field itself is so beautiful, the beautiful green and the perfect white lines. And it's so beautiful when they come together on the mound to discuss, I assume, the game of baseball and how to play it.

Being high up in the stadium is a very strange and unique sensation. There are not other situations in my life where I am viewing the world at such an angle. It is an incredible experience that I think everyone should have the experience of experiencing. I do not think enough people know about Yankee Stadium. It probably doesn't even cross their mind. I am aware that there are probably about one billion sports fans who go there, but I mean that all kinds of people should go there, on account of how mesmerizing and inspiring it is. I think painters should go watch a game of baseball at Yankee Stadium. Because then they will be very inspired to paint the baseball field.

I Love Watching Baseball on TV

Although watching the game at the stadium feels like the most perfect activity in the world, there is also something perfect about watching it on television. I love the commentators and the way that they talk about the game and the players. My favorite thing they say is, "Mama, there go that man again!"

It is also amazing that all of America is being connected by their television screens to the team and to each other. They are feeling "magic" and "luck" all together even though they are far apart. It is truly beautiful what the Yankees do for the world. It isn't easy to play baseball and it isn't easy to play it in front of so many people. They make us happy and they give us something to care about. They give us something to do. I am currently enduring a dark night of the soul that has essentially eradicated my faith, so all I can do is try to pass time.

There are lots of ways to pass time. I play pool, or do crosswords, or play Scrabble, or play chess, or I pretend, or I watch baseball. It is America's favorite pastime.

"Baseball time is sacred time. Football, hockey, soccer and basketball run by the clock. Play is constrained by the seconds and minutes of linear time. Baseball's time, though, is non-linear, relativistic, where an inning can last as little as a few minutes, or as long as an hour. Indeed, the pace of the game is determined by the motion and position of the ball."

I used to think that people who watched sports on television and got excited or angry were being performative. Or that they just wanted an excuse to scream really loudly in front of their wives. I used to think that I was better and smarter than people who liked sports. The beauty of the baseball field and the glove and the ball are what drew me to baseball; but then I started to really care about the Yankees, and I too screamed at the television and jumped and clapped and cried. When they win a game, I walk outside and get excited to see someone wearing a Yankees cap, so that we can smile at each other.

I'm Just Going to Say It: Baseball is Sexual

I was not aware of this element of the game until I saw it in person. My relationship to Anthony Volpe was purely fanatical and platonic, albeit deeply spiritual. However, when I saw him in person, there was something—quite frankly—erotic about it.

I confided this in Sargent, who was temporarily not my boyfriend due to the darkness that ensued around the time the Yankees lost because I hadn't eaten bananas. Sargent said, "It's perfectly healthy and normal for a woman to have a mild sexual fixation on a New York Yankee." He even said that the Yankees are "famously sexual" and that they "have sex." I'm confused about this because it seems to me that almost all of them are married. I am not sure if the Yankees have sexual relations with their fans.

And I wonder if they would like me sexually because I do not look or act like their other fans. And I wonder if that would actually make it more interesting for them to have sexual relations with me. I was just wondering about that.

I Ate a Hot Dog at Yankee Stadium

I ate a hot dog there.

So There's This Ball . . .

One of the most beautiful things that baseball players do with the ball is when they throw it to each other in a zig-zag sort of way after an out. Based on my research this is called "throwing around the horn." When they do this, I am reminded of how much skill they have and how easy they make it look to perfectly catch and throw a ball, of how their practice and hard work has paid off. I am also reminded of the fact that they are on a team together. I am reminded of the special and rare type of friendship that comes with being on a team. The best kind of friendship feels like being on a team together, even if you guys don't play baseball.

I have a ball with the Yankees logo on it, which was given to me by my forlorn Montrealer friend called Étienne. I play catch with the ball and sometimes I just hold it while I sleep, but I could never throw it around the horn like they do. While I watched the game in the Bronx, Etienne watched it on his television in Canada. When the Red Sox would score a point, he'd text me: "they're cheating."

Baseball Induced Mania

After I left Yankee Stadium, I went to sleep and had a horrific nightmare. Sargent said I was screaming and punching in my sleep. But when I woke up, I felt happier and more inspired and more talkative than I have in months. In fact, I could not stop talking and explained to him all of the amazing and interesting things that happened at the baseball game and all of the amazing and interesting things about baseball in general.

He read me an article by Hannah M.G. Shapero about baseball as an esoteric ritual: "For rookies, each time at bat is an initiation; for others, wielding the sacred wand can be either an ordeal or a triumph. (For the sake of brevity, I will not elaborate on the phallic aspects of this ritual, which is done only by men and only during the most fertile times of the year.)"

I told him that he would look good in a Yankees uniform and that he would look good with a bunch of dust on him. I asked him to pretend to be a Yankees player who just finished playing the game so I could gather intel on what playing the game felt like. He pretended to be really out of breath for a really long time and kept saying he had just finished the game and that's why he was so out of breath. I realized I didn't really know what to ask the Yankee except for whether the "having sex" thing was true. He told me that yes, it was true, and then we had sex.

Everyone at This Baseball Game is Kissing and Getting Married Except for Me

Three women were proposed to at Yankee Stadium. Their boyfriends paid money to write things on the big screen, like GREISY I LOVE YOU WILL YOU MARRY ME. Well, the first one said that, and the second one just said KANDIS WILL YOU MARRY ME. I thought if I was Kandis, I'd feel inferior and wonder why my boyfriend hadn't written I LOVE YOU like Greisy's boyfriend had. But it's not like Kandis' boyfriend knew that Greisy's boyfriend was gonna write that. I thought about how men who propose to their girlfriends at Yankee Stadium should have some sort of group chat where they compare their proposals, like how girls in high school have groups dedicated to making sure no one wears the same prom dress. I thought about it so hard that I didn't catch the name of the third woman getting proposed to. However, upon thinking about it even harder, I now feel that the group chat is unnecessary, because I would just be grateful to be at Yankee Stadium and to be getting proposed to in a celebration of baseball and love, and I should not compare myself to others. I am able to think this thought because I am disciplined and I have spent months thinking very hard about gratitude as well as about baseball and about love.

"Finally, baseball reminds us that there is an element of ritual in all games, and that a ritual is in itself a kind of game, played by a team within a sacred space, with special garb and implements. The outcome of a ritual, however, is not reflected on a scoreboard in hits and runs. The ritual game has a value that is far more abstract and less subject to the dualism of winning and losing. But a failure in ritual, like a loss in baseball, is not eternal: there is always next game or next year. And success in ritual, as in baseball, brings joy to a community and a whole city. It connects sacred and profane, inner and outer worlds. Ritual is sacred play, which brings cosmic inspiration to its participants on common ground."

My Baseball Fantasy

I walk to Yankee Stadium at night. It is dark and stormy and the Yankees are playing against the Red Sox. The Yankees win because they score twenty home runs. Because the Red Sox are cheating, they are arrested and thrown in jail. There is blood all over the baseball field and broken bats all over the baseball field, too. The reason there is blood and broken bats everywhere is because Anthony Volpe and Aaron Judge beat the Red Sox horribly with their bats before the Red Sox were all taken to jail. The police actually encouraged and allowed it because we have a new Mayor in New York City who is very woke and erotic and interested in righteous violence especially when it pertains to baseball. He is also very against graffiti.

Everyone left Yankee Stadium because it was their bedtime but I am really mature and disciplined so the Mayor said I can go to bed whenever I want, so I am the only person here. I run down to the field and trip over a baseball.

"Sorry," Anthony smiles. "That's my ball."

I look up from the ground, my skintight black gothic dress covered in baseball dirt. "This is so embarrassing," I mutter. "My skintight black gothic dress is all covered in baseball dirt."

Anthony takes off his jersey with the number 11 on the back. "You can wear this," he says, exposing his bare chest, sweating because he has just finished the game and so he is really hot and also out of breath.

I jump up in shock as he drapes the jersey over my frail body which is also soaking wet from the rain because it is a dark and stormy night. "Let's get you dry," he says, leading me to the dugout where Aaron Judge is also sitting.

Aaron gives me a big beautiful smile. "Hi, Kathy," he says.

I blush and tuck a lock of wet blonde hair behind my ear. "H-how did you know my name, Mr. Judge?"

"We all know your name. You are the number one fan of the Yankees."

"Yeah, that is true," I say. "I am well-known in New York for being a sexually submissive Yankees fan. And what's important about that is these are two separate parts of my personality that are allowed to exist simultaneously and there's nothing wrong with being who I am. I'm just me."

"Okay," Aaron says. "That's really true. By the way I wanted to tell you that a few years ago me and Anthony Volpe, and every other member of the Yankees, all of our wives and families died in a horrible fire accident. So we are not married and we don't have families. But since it was years ago, we have had a sufficient amount of time to grieve, and also our wives always said they wanted us to be able to experiment with our sexuality freely and without guilt if they were to ever die."

I look around the baseball field, thinking about baseball. "I hear you, Aaron. Thank you for letting me know. And I'm sorry for your loss."

"I'm sorry too," Anthony says. "It is an unimaginable loss that no one should ever have to go through. But one thing I have learned is that in life, you lose. Both in baseball and in love.

You lose the things you care about the most and there's nothing you can do to stop it. All you can do is keep going."

I start to cry. "Anthony, you don't know how much those words mean to me. I have lost so much. And I just want to love again. I miss my lover. My . . . my teammate."

"You really loved him, huh," Aaron says, tapping his bat against the ground. "Well . . . we can be your teammates tonight," he grins, gripping the bat tightly and moaning and Anthony starts to moan also.

"R-really?" I stutter, so overwhelmed that I fall to the ground again. Now my black gothic fishnets are covered in baseball dirt and I scrape my knees while helplessly tumbling over a broken baseball bat and there is blood coming out of my knees.

"The blood coming out of your knees is very . . . gothic," Anthony remarks with a smirk.

"Oh, *that* . . ." I whisper, blushing uncontrollably. "I wasn't sure how you guys felt about gothic Yankees fans," I say, nervously digging my black kitten heels into the dirt. "I was nervous about it, you know . . . all of your fans are . . . they're . . . they're preps, okay? They're preps and they're jocks, and I'm just a geeky nerdy girl with a laptop and a dream. I mean, how would a member of the New York Yankees ever be attracted to me? I'm just . . . stupid! *Stupid stupid stupid!*"

Anthony and Aaron laugh. "You're not stupid," they say.

"Then what am I?" I shout into the sky of Yankee Stadium, tears and rain falling down my cheeks.

"You're . . . *beautiful*," Anthony says, grabbing my arm with his baseball glove and staring into my Yankee-blue eyes.

Aaron stands over me with his tall baseball

body as the rain suddenly stops and the sun comes out even though it is nighttime. It shines over the beautiful green baseball grass and a soft breeze encompasses the three of us. I run my shaking fingers over the leather of the glove wrapped tightly around Anthony's strong hand. He pushes me to the ground and I gasp in shock. Anthony and Aaron carry me to the mound, the place they typically gather to discuss baseball and how it is played. They pin me down. Gripping my thrashing gothic hips, Anthony hovers his mouth over mine. He leans in and kisses my whimpering mouth. I allow it to happen for a moment before slowly pushing him off of me.

"I'm sorry," I say. "I just don't know if I can do this." I look up and see Aaron's enormous engorged member visibly throbbing through his baseball pants. "As enticing as your visibly throbbing member is, I just don't know if I'm ready for this experience. I know you said we're a team, but . . . I miss my real teammate. We had this sexual encounter in Starbucks. You may have heard a rumor about it . . . ?"

"Yes, we did. He entered your small hot wet mouth at Starbucks, right?"

"Yeah."

"Well, we know how hard it is to move on. We told you about the horrible accident and the fire involving our families."

"Thanks for understanding," I say.

"Of course we understand," Anthony says, his shining eyes peering out from under his New York Yankees baseball cap.

"And hey, Kathy?"

"Yeah?"

"Keep the jersey."

CHRISTMAS

When I was a kid, I used to get so excited about Christmas that I'd throw up every Christmas Eve. I would be so excited and nervous and freaked out about Santa coming that I would be throwing up all night long.

Once, my mother thought I was done being sick for the night, so she placed a bow on the trumpet she'd gotten me and placed it in my bedroom. She got me a trumpet because I played the trumpet and I was very good at it. I woke up to vomit again and I was so sick I didn't see the trumpet. But when I returned to my room I rubbed my eyes and I saw it. I was so overcome with joy and gratitude and shock that I started crying and ran back to the bathroom to throw up more.

I always wondered how it could be possible for Santa to know me so well. I would thank my mother for the gifts she had gotten me, but I would admit that Santa had gotten me better ones. If I were her, I wouldn't have been able to take it. I would have been extremely jealous of Santa.

When I found out the Easter Bunny wasn't real and that it was really my mother, I wept for hours. I drew an image of my mother as the Grim Reaper cracking open Easter eggs with a scythe.

"How could you lie to me?" I begged. "For all these years, how?"

She laughed. She thought it was funny that my grief arose not from the dematerialization of the Easter Bunny, but from being lied to; as if lying were an ultimate, unforgivable crime. And it kind of is. But she was always fond of lying.

• • •

"I'M WORRIED ABOUT letting Christmas down," I say to my therapist. "Does that make sense?"

"Mmm. No," she says.

I swear to God, every session, she tells me to get an air fryer. I don't know why she thinks getting an air fryer will save me. Getting an air fryer and going to Walmart. Those are the two things she's always telling me to do.

I'm worried about Christmas because it's like when you're on vacation and you feel pressured to have fun. I feel pressured by the spirit of Christmas to have an amazing Christmas. But this might be the first Christmas I spend alone.

Christmas is so important to me that it's how I escaped the pedophile's house back in California when I was a teenager. I absolutely had to go home for Christmas. We bought a ticket for me to go back to New York for a few days and then return to Pedophile Pizza Hut House (he worked at Pizza Hut). And no, I'm not saying he's a pedophile for having sexual relations with me when I was sixteen, that's its own issue, he confided in me that he was an actual pedophile, like actual kids, it's a whole thing, I don't want to talk about it anymore. He had serious issues. I think he killed himself. No one can find him.

But I came home to New York for Christmas and then I never went back.

• • •

THERE'S SOMETHING ABOUT spending Christmas alone that I'm drawn to because I have a victim complex. But there's no good in Christmas if there's no tree. If I spend Christmas alone,

I need to acquire a tree. Christmas is all about staring at the Christmas tree while listening to Christmas music. It is also about decorating the Christmas tree. And it is about exchanging gifts in the presence of the Christmas tree. If I were a prostitute, I could afford the Christmas tree.

Morg was introducing me to some of her friends. This one works in film, this one works in whatever. Then they're looking at me. "What does Kathy do?" one of them says.

Morg pauses for a long time. "Kathy is a really . . . really . . . interesting person."

• • •

PART OF WHY I want to go to my mother's for Christmas is because of the star on the tree. When my stepfather came and lived with us and ruined our house and our lives, he also brought a light-up angel tree-topper from Guatemala.

I was very upset because everyone knows that stars are what go on top of Christmas trees. It was very disrespectful towards Christmas in my opinion.

After all the Child Protective Services stuff, after he was gone, I gathered my three sisters, two of them Guatemalan, into the kitchen with me. I had us make a paper mâché star. We sculpted it and painted it gold. Every year after that, it went on top of the tree.

It reminds me of this ring my mother had. It was gold and had gemstones in it, one representing the birth month of everyone in our family: my stepfather, my three sisters, and me. One day, she lost it. She was really torn up about it. I was torn up, too. I asked my grandmother to take me to the jeweler's. I designed a new and better ring: one with only the gemstones representing the birth months of me and my three sisters. My mother cried when I presented it to her. I am not sure if they were tears of joy.

• • •

WHENEVER I HAVE SEX, I'm convinced that the man's "area" is going to injure my "area." I have to talk myself down before, during, and after the act.

I've been this way since I was a kid. The inside of my body freaks me out. I used to wake up from night terrors screaming and hallucinating about blood and veins. You'd think getting molested gives you nightmares solely about getting molested. But it also gives you nightmares about stuff like getting your head cut off and watching your friends get their heads cut off.

When I lost my virginity, I bled. I looked in the bathroom mirror and I thought I'd see myself really different. Like I would be an adult. But I wasn't. I was just scared. The bathroom was filled with cobwebs.

The only time I really thought I looked like an adult was after I did heroin for the first time. I was on the train home from my ex-boyfriend's apartment and I saw my reflection in the window. I looked old, sick, and sad. I looked hopeless. I thought, "I'll never be the same." It was a horrifying thought. The truth is that it wasn't the end of the world and I only ended up doing heroin a few more times, just to make sure that I was doing it right. It just wasn't for me. But my boyfriend really loved it. It's like he was addicted to it or something.

The worst thing I've ever seen is probably when he overdosed. I was playing *Hotline Miami* in his living room while he was in the bathroom. I didn't know he was using. He was supposed to be clean. It's true that I'd been having to nudge him awake while we played video games, but I didn't want to make a big deal about it.

I heard a noise like the one from *The Grudge* coming from the bathroom. Like gurgling and clicking and moaning. I let it happen for a little while, figuring if I was making those noises in the bathroom, I wouldn't want to be bothered. But after a minute or so, it seemed too weird.

"Andrew?" I called out. "Are you okay?" He didn't say anything. Nothing. Just more gurgling.

"Andrew? It's not funny. Can you stop?" I knocked on the door, hard. Still nothing. "If you don't stop I'm going to come in there. I don't care what you're doing." Nothing. "Okay, I'm coming in."

I don't know what I did to deserve God's grace in ensuring the door was unlocked. Andrew's head was wedged between the toilet and the sink. His face was a purplish-blue. I screamed.

It still didn't hit me that he had overdosed.

I was too horrified by his dying face and dying body to notice the needle on the ground or the heroin on the counter. I thought it was some freak seizure. I moved like a robot or a marionette, calling 911 and running to his mother's apartment door, banging and screaming "HELP ANDREW IS DYING," running back to Andrew's apartment, screaming at his body, begging the paramedics to come faster, repeating his address over and over again, begging him to stop, hoping this was a cruel but impressively elaborate joke.

I tried to un-wedge his head. I kept weakening, worried that I was breaking his neck. He wouldn't be able to scream or cry if I were hurting him. He'd just continue rolling his eyes back into his purple head.

"Get him on his side," the 911 operator said—or maybe it was on his back. Everything was too loud. Whatever he told me to do, I did it.

His mother found the needle. "Should I use Narcan?" I screamed. "He said to use Narcan!"

"Uh . . . I don't know what that is," the operator said. "Don't do anything. Just wait for them to come."

A silent neighbor stood outside of the apartment door I had propped open in preparation for someone to save my dying boyfriend. He watched me scream.

"Either try to calm down or give the phone to someone else," the operator said. I gave the phone to Andrew's mother, refusing to calm down. When the paramedics got there they dragged Andrew's body from the bathroom into the living room. *Hotline Miami* was still on the television.

I stood on the couch, screaming, "PLEASE WAKE UP! PLEASE WAKE UP! PLEASE WAKE UP!"

They gave him Narcan. Nothing happened. "WAKE UP! WAKE UP! WAKE UP! WAKE UP!"

They gave him CPR. They did it for maybe a minute. Then they did it for another minute.

"WAKE UP! WAKE UP! WAKE UP! WAKE UP!"

Andrew groaned.

Andrew was still high when we got to the ER. He was trying to make out with me. I'd told the doctor that I was his sister in fear that she wouldn't let me in the room if we weren't related. I shrugged in her direction when he started fondling me.

Andrew's mother brought me a bacon egg and cheese. I ate it in the lobby even though I was a vegetarian. I put it into my mouth the same way you put a CD into a CD player.

I took the train home like I did the first time I'd done heroin. When I saw my reflection, I had the same feeling that I wasn't the same. This time it was true.

• • •

I FIND A twenty dollar bill in my bag. I'd gotten a new vape a few days ago, but I'd gone to a lousy store that only had lousy flavors. When something tastes bad, it tastes even worse when you realize you don't have the money to replace it with something that tastes good. But I find twenty dollars. Exactly enough for a new one.

At the bodega, I see this beautiful big package of Twizzlers. Black licorice Twizzlers. I've never seen them before. I'm so excited. I love black licorice and I love Twizzlers. It feels like a Christmas miracle. I remove them from the shelf and I hold them in my hands and I wait in line.

When it's my turn, I say, "Okay, how much are these?"

"Three ninety-nine," Hassan says.

"Okay. And how much are these?" I ask, pointing to the vapes.

"I give it to you for fifteen."

I pull out the twenty dollar bill. "So this is enough for all of it then?"

"Mmm-hmm!" Hassan says.

"Wow, perfect," a man in the sandwich line says.

"It's just for you. You don't tell anyone about that!" Hassan says, smiling. I bring my hand up to my mouth, zip it, lock it, and put it in my pocket. He gives me back a lucky dollar.

When I was a kid, I thought that "zip it, lock it, throw it out the window" was a lot smarter, because if the key is in your pocket, you can easily retrieve it and unzip your lip, which completely ruins the whole concept of zipping and locking it in the first place.

"Happy holiday," Hassan says, and I wonder if he thinks I'm Jewish. I consider saying "Merry Christmas" back to him, but I think he's Muslim, and I don't want to act aggressive. But the

Christmas spirit is for everyone, not just Christians, and so I say, "You too." The Christmas spirit courses through my body and I jump up and down with my licorice and my vape. If Santa Claus or his wife said to me, "Kathy, you're a Christmas girl," I'd experience something similar to gender euphoria.

My whole life revolves around Christmas. I think everyone's does. We're just sitting around every year, waiting for Christmas to come. And it's about to come. Thank you everyone for putting up amazing Christmas lights and decorations. You are keeping everyone alive.

• • •

I TRY THE black licorice Twizzlers. Disappointing. Kind of a rancid flavor or something. It's the vape all over again. The smell of them is actually making me sick. I'll have to throw them away.

What an absolute tragedy. It's almost enough to make me lose hope in life completely. I guess that's the issue with being salvational about Twizzlers.

I won't buy new ones. A dollar isn't enough for new ones, and it's a lucky dollar anyhow. I'll just listen to *The Beach Boys' Christmas Album* over and over and over again. I'll listen especially close to the part at the end:

Hi, this is Denny, and speaking for the rest of the guys, I'd like to say that it has been a great pleasure for all of us to bring you this Christmas album. We hope you will treasure it the way we do. And if you happen to be listening to this album right now, Mike, Brian, Carl, Al and I would like to wish every one of you a very merry Christmas, and we hope the new year brings you as much happiness as this year has brought us. Thank you very much.

A Story About Christmas

Here is a story about Christmas:

It is Christmas Day and it is snowing so much. I'm on my way to a trendy cafe to meet up with Axel, my boyfriend. He is 22-years-old and he is woke and he has spiky brown hair with black streaks in it and an eyebrow piercing with a green sparkly weed leaf dangling off it because he smokes weed. The cafe is called Starbucks.

We go into the bathroom of Starbucks and start popping pills because we are pill poppers and we like to get high on pills. It's cool, giving someone a drug then taking some and getting high off it. Axel starts smoking weed out of a bong in the bathroom at Starbucks and says, "I'm getting so high off this kush."

"That's so cool and sexy of you," I murmur, letting my eyes close for a moment. I reach into my bag and retrieve some of the heroin that hurts. It's like normal heroin, but instead of making you feel good, it really hurts. Me and my boyfriend are addicted to it. I inject half a syringe of the heroin that hurts into my arm and then I pull it out and inject the rest into Axel's arm. We start feeling immense pain inside the Starbucks bathroom and we are obsessed with how painful it feels because we are gothic.

We leave the bathroom and head to the counter. The combination of pills and kush and the heroin that hurts makes the Starbucks menu look so . . . trippy. Admiring the kaleidoscope of festive beverage offerings, I order a Tall Gingerbread Oatmilk Chai and Axel orders a Venti Peppermint Mocha. I see a snowman cookie in the display case and I ask the barista for one of those as well.

"Don't order that," Axel growls at me, his grip

tightening around his seasonal beverage, crushing it with his immense strength.

"Why?" I ask, as black angel wings sprout out of his back and he starts crying blood.

"Eating cookies from Starbucks is ghetto and ratchet," he hisses wokely. "You should only purchase cookies from local bakeries." His sharp vampire teeth shine under the moody Starbucks light. Axel coaxes me into the darkest corner of Starbucks and brushes my bangs aside. He pins me against the wall and my Gingerbread Oatmilk Chai flies into the air and splatters all over the rustic tiled floor. He pulls down his black skinny jeans and thrusts his enormous throbbing gothic member into my private area as I gasp in shock.

"That escalated quickly," a queer person of color peering into our dark world remarks, chuckling and finishing off the last sip of his

Trenta Cran-Merry Orange Refresher, typing furiously onto his 12" M2 16GB MacBook Air.

The barista starts hooting and hollering and asking what the ruckus is all about. Axel ignores his cries, the same way he ignores my whimpers, forcing his hand over my mouth and continuing to make rough, passionate love to my body.

The barista walks over to the shadowy, sexual corner of Starbucks. He shrieks in pain. "I am horrifically furious with you," he says. "I am non-binary and I am woke, and I am going to call the police." I start to scream from fear, but Axel pushes his strong hand even harder against my small, hot, wet mouth, causing me to sexually climax uncontrollably.

"I myself have something of a gendered past," Axel growls at the barista as he continues thrusting into me, his pace quickening as his rage grows. "And woke, you say?" He chuckles. "Woke, woke, woke . . . you don't know the meaning of woke. Woke = healing my girlfriend's sexual trauma by fucking her hard (with penetration) at Starbucks, her favorite trendy cafe. Woke is me. Woke is my girlfriend. Woke is US," he bellows, before looking the barista dead in the eyes and howling: "Calling the police is NOT woke."

I gasp as Axel flings my body against the communal wooden table, no longer hiding our love in the shadows, sinking his vampire fangs into my neck.

"Okay you just gagged him," I say to Axel in between moans, thinking to myself, *this chile just spilled the tea*.

"That's not the only thing I'm going to spill," he warns me with a grin, taunting me with his vampire mind-reading abilities. Axel removes a double-barreled shotgun, which is the same size as his member, from the waistband of his black skinny jeans and shoots the barista to death.

This only infuriates the barista further. There is my blood and barista blood and seasonal beverages spilled all over the floor as Axel spills his dark vampiric seed into me and his eyes turn red and my eyes also turn red.

We head back into the bathroom of Starbucks. I work on some stuff on my MacBook while Axel crushes up an Adderall and snorts it.

"What are you working on?" he asks.

"Just a story," I say. "A story about Christmas. A story about love. A story about, well . . . a story about today. This has been the greatest day of my life." I smile, looking up from my MacBook into his glowing red eyes. "It's just a story," I repeat. "A story . . . about us."

VIDEO GAMES

My old coworker Carter who had a foot fetish and who was recovering from a heroin addiction—he had a big crush on me. I thought he was cute in a sort of demented way when I first met him. He had hair like Beck and he wore striped sweaters from 2007 and skinny jeans from 2007. I led him on.

He was lanky and sad and tired no matter how much he slept. He was cold to everyone but me. We liked the same music and when we worked shifts together he would be impressed by my album choices. I would be impressed by him being impressed by my album choices.

When a customer traded in a bunch of old

consoles and games worth a bunch of money, I'd have to call Carter and ask him how to write a check. My hands would be shaking and I would be red in the face. I'd be so sweaty that my shirt would be wet and I would scribble numbers on a piece of paper, standing across from an equally sweaty man waiting to get paid. Carter was the only one who knew how to write checks. He was the oldest. He was the smartest. That's why I latched onto him.

He quickly got too obsessed with me. So did his boss, who was also Carter's best friend, and who was also a recovering heroin addict. But to my knowledge, he didn't have a foot fetish.

"You're the first woman to ever work here!" his boss said. I jumped and clapped my hands together from how excited I was. I was not smart enough to realize that this was not a good thing.

• • •

WHEN I MOVED TO Connecticut, my roommate drove us around and we saw the video game store for the first time. I asked her to pull over so we could go inside. I thought it totally ruled and I bought my favorite Scooby Doo GameCube game.

I'd never had a job before. My roommate said, "Ask them if they're hiring." I said, "I'm too shy." She said, "Okay, then I'll ask."

They told her to come back the next day when the boss would be there. So I showed up the next day. I hoped they would not notice that I was Kathy, and not my lesbian roommate who wore fingerless gloves. They did not notice. The boss asked me what video games I liked.

"*LSD Dream Emulator, Hotline Miami, Super Mario Sunshine, Super Smash Bros Melee, Skyrim*—"

"You can stop. I was just checking that you weren't gonna say any sports games."

I told him I was a freak who never had a real job and that I had a bunch of mental issues but I would try my best to be a good worker.

He hired me on the spot. He really believed in me. I felt really happy. I studied hard and wrote extensive color-coded notes on all the videos he told me to watch.

• • •

CARTER USED TO TRY to convince me to take off my shoes and socks in front of him. I would never do it. I would never take off my socks in public. I actually think I would more readily show someone my breasts.

My boss asked me if the reason I slouched so much was to "hide my knockers." I said, "Um, yeah." He asked me "what was up" with my necklace and if I was "religious or something." I said, "Um, yeah," and wondered if it was illegal for him to ask me that.

Once he said, "What would you do if I just grabbed you by the neck and pinned you against the wall?" and I said, "Um, I would ask you to stop, I guess."

It reminded me of how when I was fourteen at summer camp in the Catskills, one of the camp counselors did that to me. In the middle of a film class, he just pinned me to the wall by my throat. As a joke. He was kind of crazed and grunting. But he was handsome and intelligent and nobody knew what to do so they just laughed. I felt like it might mean that I was pretty or important for him to do that to me. But I also felt scared. I went on a hunger strike and was sent home early.

. . .

WORKING AT A JOB is really scary. It requires a lot of benzodiazepines and cigarette breaks. But it's fun when you're putting labels on game cases. It's fun to make them lined up just right. It's fun when a customer comes in and says: "I'd like to buy the stupidest game you have." And you're like, "Oh, I saw this one game . . . here it is! *Big Mutha Truckers* . . ."

. . .

ONE NIGHT Carter came over and we watched *Boogie Nights*. He kept trying to touch me. I kept doing cocaine, which was the only thing to do in Connecticut, and saying "no" whenever he got too close to me. He said, "This movie makes me want to fuck." I said, "Oh. Really? This movie just makes me want to do cocaine."

Once he said he wanted to jump my bones. I thought that meant he wanted to murder me. I thought he wanted to murder me because he was annoyed at me for being annoying and for making too many mistakes at work. I recently found out it meant he wanted to have sex with me but in my experience having sex doesn't involve jumping and it doesn't involve that many bones either.

Once Carter took me to his friend Kevin's house. Kevin showed me his gun and his *Ghost in the Shell* poster. It was dark so he lit up the poster with the tactical light on the gun. I was impressed and a little concerned about him shooting me but I didn't have that much to live for.

Kevin made us pizza. He dropped it on the floor and we ate it anyway. Kevin said a lot of racial slurs. He was a drunk. His bathroom had a Putin calendar in it.

I was hesitant about eating the pizza not because it had been dropped on the floor but because I was obsessed with my weight because I was having a lot of problems in my life. Carter told Kevin that I thought I was fat. Kevin said that I was not fat and that I should eat the pizza, then pulled out his phone to show me an image of a dead disfigured man in a car wreck. Carter told Kevin I thought I was ugly. Kevin brought a cigarette to his mouth, lit it, and said, "You look like one of them Boticelli chicks."

Kevin was the only one who knew how to fix game consoles. He didn't technically work at the store, but he would come in drunk and slurring (drunk-slurring and racial-slurring) and he'd fix some joy-cons on a Nintendo Switch and then get kicked out. It seemed like he would somehow manifest a customer of whatever race he was ragging on and we'd be like "Dude stop stop stop stop stop stop stop stop stop stop sto—hi, how's it going . . ."

• • •

ON MY BIRTHDAY, I had no friends. I had moved to this shitty Connecticut town to be with my boyfriend but he ended up being more interested in a sixteen-year-old girl he met online. It's funny how history repeats itself considering my first boyfriend was an adult man I met online when I was sixteen. But now I was turning twenty-one.

My boss was really nice about it. I took a day off and when I came back to work I was crying at the cash register. He told me I was a sweet girl and that I didn't deserve this.

He offered to take me to eat some birthday

dinner and drink a birthday beer. I was telling him about that Gypsy Rose Blanchard show over some Greek food. I talked about how uncomfortable it was to watch the e-sex scenes.

"I bet you're into that," he said. "What?"

"I bet you're into, like, BDSM. I bet you're into petplay," he said, without looking up from his food.

"I'm not."

"You are," he said.

I felt humiliated and caught even though "petplay" wasn't one of my deviances. Sex isn't the time to "play." It's not a laughing matter.

"My girlfriend is into that stuff," he continued. "She's always saying I'm not rough enough with her. But one night, when I was really mad at her, I raped her for real. She was crying. But it's like, she got what she wanted."

"Oh, nice."

I continued ripping my pita into bite-sized pieces but didn't put any of them into my mouth.

On the drive home, he gave me a cupcake out of a container that contained two cupcakes.

"The other one's for my girlfriend," he said.

"Nice."

• • •

ONE DAY I WAS looking at the poster in the back room at the video game store. It was faded but you could still make out some of the words on it, about sexual harassment and stuff, and what to do if your boss seems strange. I squinted at it. My boss elbowed open the door and stared at me.

"What are you doing?" he asked.

"Nothing. Chilling."

I stayed late in the back room while he

explained his movie idea to me. He must have explained it to me for about two hours. I kept saying things like, "Oh, wow, well it sounds really good," and motioning for us to leave the store. But then he'd say, "Well that's not even the best part." The plot was about exacting revenge on his ex-girlfriend but it also involved him being a superhero. And it went on for so long that tears started to form in my eyes. I typically don't experience boredom, but for the first time in my life I started to cry from how bored I was. My boss smiled and said, "Yeah. Every time I explain my movie to someone, it makes them cry."

• • •

ONE DAY me and Carter and my boss were at the skatepark. An older man walked over and started taking pictures of me. He said, "Great face. Great hair." I was afraid he was either making fun of me or capturing material to jack off to and I spent some time trying to calculate which option was worse.

Carter knew I hated getting my photo taken. I kept covering my face and mumbling.

"She doesn't like that, man," he said. "She doesn't like pictures."

The man stopped taking pictures. "But she's beautiful," he said.

"We know," Carter said. "We keep telling her. But she doesn't like pictures." The man listened to Carter. I felt grateful for Carter. I felt like Carter was a knight in shining armor.

A kid skated up to me and said, "I'm a Pisces. What's your number?" So of course I gave it to him immediately.

Carter saw the whole thing. I guess he was jealous. I guess he had just saved my life.

My boss gave me a ride home. He scolded me

about giving the Pisces my number. He yelled. He said it was unfair to Carter. I was sobbing in the car.

He eventually started to feel empathy and pulled over to a liquor store. I bought beer and got drunk and stopped crying. You can drink beer in the passenger seat in Connecticut.

"I don't like being around you when you're drunk," my boss said.

I don't like being around you *ever*, I thought.

Unforgiven

I am crying in the rain and screaming in the parking lot of the store I work at. I am crying because I am homeless and because I just got fired from the store.

"Why are you crying?" A dark figure asks.

"I am crying because I am homeless and because I just got fired from the store," I say.

The dark figure tips his hat. "Homelessness is wrong," he whispers.

"Yes, I agree with you." Underneath his hat I can see something sparkling. "Don't come any closer," I shriek. "My ex-boyfriend had an eyebrow piercing with a sparkly green weed leaf on it. He wore it because he smoked weed," I sob. I rip my matching sparkly green weed leaf necklace off of my neck and throw it onto the wet pavement.

"I'm not your ex-boyfriend," the figure says.

"Then why are black angel wings sprouting out of your back and why are you crying blood?" I ask. "You must be Axel, my gothic 22-year-old ex-boyfriend."

The figure chuckles and stamps his swisher sweet out on the ground. "I am twenty-two," he says. He walks closer, touching his private zone in a horrifically inappropriate way as he does so. "And my name is Axel."

I begin to scream and shout from pain and

trauma. I start to run into the woods. My tears are black because I am wearing a lot of black eyeliner and mascara because I am gothic and my thighs are bleeding because I cut myself because I have emotional problems.

"Not so fast," Axel growls, descending from the sky with his giant black wings and grabbing me by my small waist. "You didn't let me finish."

I stand there, limp, unable to escape his grip. "Then finish," I whimper, as he pushes aside my black and grey striped underwear which I have paired with matching black and grey striped thigh-high socks.

Axel smirks. "I am not your ex-boyfriend."

He pauses for a moment, glaring at me before exclaiming, "I am actually your boyfriend and also we are dating," and then he sinks his vampire teeth into my neck and drinks my blood.

"Okay I literally feel so confused right now,"

I say. "How can this be? What about the Battle of Bushwick?"

The Battle of Bushwick was a two-month long war which happened in Bushwick. The battle was fought between me, a geeky nerd, and my gothic hacker boyfriend Axel. There was a tremendous amount of bloodshed and the FBI came and ICE came which infuriated Axel due to his wokeness.

"That was a long war," he sighs. "But not in vampire years." A dead rose with thorns on it floats onto the ground. He whimpers before picking it up and crushing it with his immense strength.

Axel lights a joint and does a bunch of tricks with the weed smoke. "I've punished you sufficiently for your war crimes," he speaks while exhaling. "I sent a hundred werewolves to scare you every night."

"Right that was so scary."

"But if you really want me to be your boyfriend . . . there's one more thing I have to do," he grunts. Then he pulls out a branding iron from the tool belt attached to his black and white studded belt and he brands me on my pale white back. I scream horrifically. I pull out my iPhone 13 to snap a pic of the markings on my back. On the top of my back it says "Unforgiven" in Edwardian Script ITC. Then there is a red circle with a line through it crossing out the word "Unforgiven." Then under that it says "NEVER AGAIN" in all-caps Palatino. Then "NEVER AGAIN" is crossed out with a straight line. Then under that it says "One Last Chance" in Freestyle Script. Next to that there is two paw prints and a lipstick kiss tattooed on my lower back because Axel is a tattoo artist and he was also tattooing me as he branded me.

"So you . . . forgive me?" I whisper into the

darkness, a cool breeze flowing between me and Axel's lips.

"No," Axel howls.

I begin to cry and say that I am so sorry. "I wish I could take back all of the things I did in that battle, Axel," I say. "But I can't. And if you can't forgive me, then why don't you just shoot me? Shoot me like you shot that barista." I reach for the double-barreled shotgun stuffed in his waistband.

"Not so fast," says Anthony Volpe from the New York Yankees.

"A-Anthony?" I gasp.

Axel attempts to shoot Anthony Volpe with the shotgun, but Anthony deflects the blast with his baseball bat.

"There is no need to shoot me to death with a gun," Anthony says. "I am not here to make love to your girlfriend. And it's not because we aren't attracted to each other. We are actually extremely attracted to each other. However she doesn't feel comfortable having sex with me because she only wants to have sex with you. And I respect boundaries and consent."

I blush and cover my face because I am so shy.

"Then why are you here," Axel hisses.

"I'm here because I know that Kathy is sorry. We all make mistakes. Both of you have. And guess what? I have too. I make errors sometimes when I am playing baseball. But the beautiful thing about baseball is that you just keep going. People bully me online because they are jealous of my boyish good looks and charm. They say that I am bad at baseball and ruining the New York Yankees."

"Don't listen to them, Anthony!" I scream.

"I don't," Anthony smiles. "I can't. If I listened to everything those people said about me, I wouldn't be able to play baseball. I wouldn't be able to make you and all the other fans of the New York Yankees smile and clap when I hit the ball."

Anthony wraps his white angel wings around me and caresses my face. "Can I tell you something, Kathy?"

"Of course, Anthony. You can tell me anything."

"I wanted to tell you a secret fact about baseball. The fact is that throwing the ball is just as important as hitting the ball. Pitchers have to throw the ball at the hitbox of the batter. They can't just go throwing the ball around all willy-nilly."

Anthony hands a ball to Axel. "Feel free to crush it with your immense strength," Anthony says, so Axel goes ahead and does that.

"It's unfair that no matter how good you are at throwing the ball that a batter can just hit it," I sigh, crossing my arms and letting my bangs fall in front my eyes.

"Nothing in life is fair," says Anthony Volpe

of the New York Yankees, "especially in love and baseball. But true love is about forgiveness. A real Yankees fan forgives their favorite player for making an error."

Now Anthony hands me a baseball. "Give me your best throw, Kathy," he says softly. I wipe my tears and I throw the ball. Anthony hits a home run.

"What I'm trying to say is this; no matter which way you throw the ball, you might feel like you're letting your team down. You might feel ashamed and embarrassed."

"I feel really ashamed and embarrassed of myself," I sob.

"I know, Kathy. Sometimes I do too. You know who else did? Jesus Christ."

"Oh yeah, I heard that when Jesus Christ was carrying that cross all around the town, that for a moment he felt really ashamed because he thought that he was letting everyone down. And he almost gave up his faith in God. But then he didn't."

"Exactly," Anthony says. "He persevered. Just like pitchers do. They throw the ball. They throw it hard."

Axel's downcast eyes turn upwards to look at me and Anthony. At this point me and Anthony are sitting on a cloud and there is a rainbow behind us. Axel's eyes turn red, which is vampire code for "love."

Anthony adjusts his baseball cap and fixes his gaze on Axel. "You sent one hundred werewolves to her house every night, man."

"OKAY!" Axel screams at the moon. "I do love her and I do forgive her. I just didn't want to say that because I'm emo and gothic," he bellows. I look at him, totally stunned from shock.

"I'll let you two take it from here," Anthony winks. He uses his soft white wings to fly all the way back to Yankee Stadium.

"Axel . . . was that true?" I gasp, sprinting into his arms and burying my face into his muscular chest. "You . . . love me?"

"Not only do I love you," he growls,"but I am going to take you to Variety Coffee."

My knees go weak. Variety Coffee recently became my favorite trendy café. "A- Axel . . . " I stutter, " . . . how did you know?"

"I know everything," he says. "Not only can I read your mind, but I studied at a college."

"Oh, wow."

Axel flies into the air, holding me in his arms as we soar towards Variety Coffee. His large, ominous member throbs against my freshly burnt up back. The mixture of pleasure and pain is extremely erotic.

"There it is," he says, and shoots down into Variety Coffee and a bunch of fire is coming out of him.

Before I can even place my order with the

LGBTQ+ barista, Axel begins shoving his enormous member into my small mouth. No one at Variety Coffee really cares because they are really chill. Everyone is complimenting my new burnt up back and tattoos. I keep trying to say "thank you," but my mouth is filled with his huge frightening gothic private part and I am gagging on it gothically.

"Okay here is the coffee that you ordered," the LGBTQ+ barista says to one of the customers. "But also, something really interesting is happening inside of this store," he continues. "I was just thinking of something interesting." Axel stops thrusting his enormous member into my tight wet throat to listen to the barista's thoughts. "I was thinking about how that gothic customer is basically forcing his girlfriend into this sexual situation at Variety Coffee and that means she don't have to feel any guilt or shame about it." Then Axel puts his private zone in my private zone and we both climax at Variety Coffee and I get pregnant from that.

All the baristas cheer for us and Axel orders iced almond lattes for everyone. He doesn't let me have any because we are in an abusive relationship where he starves me.

Axel lunges at me and begins beating me because we're in an abusive relationship. "Oh I forgot that you were homeless," he says while beating me. "I am going to adopt you and abuse you mercilessly in my dungeon."

A bunch of fire starts coming out of his body again and we fly to his apartment. "You're safe here," he says, holding me inside his wings and blindfolding me and binding my wrists and chaining my helpless body to the wall.

I manage to reach into my bag and pull out a syringe of the heroin that hurts. Axel smiles.

"Kathy . . . " he breathes into my mouth, readying his forearm. "You haven't changed."

"Actually, I have changed. I have gotten more mature which granted me special privileges from Mayor Adams," I blush as Axel gazes at me with his glowing red eyes and bares his fangs.

"This whole experience . . . " I continue, "The battle, and everything I learned from it . . . it reminds me of how in *Bloodborne*, when you know too much stuff about the world, you go insane and you die. But you can also use that knowledge as currency. You use it to buy items that help others. That's why I bought this heroin that hurts." I inject the syringe into Axel's arm as he screams in pain.

"You can change even more," Axel breathes, hovering his mouth over my neck. "I can turn you into a vampire. You can have glowing red eyes and you can cry blood and fire can come out of you." He holds my head in his hands. "And you can have black angel wings. And we can fly. We can fly to Variety Coffee." Extremely high on kush and heroin, he clasps a brand new sparkly green weed leaf necklace around my neck as we kiss each other.

I reach into my pocket and pull out a slice of pumpkin loaf. Axel recoils in disgust. "That does not look like it is from a local bakery," he growls.

"Actually, it is from a local bakery. You may have heard of it; it's called Variety Coffee."

Axel gasps in shock.

"While you weren't looking, I stealthily purchased this baked good from the LGBTQ+ barista at Variety Coffee. You weren't looking because you were pushing your incredibly large member into my warm mouth as I choked and whimpered from arousal."

"But you can't eat it," Axel protests, slamming his fist against the wall as his eyes turn black. "We are in an abusive relationship where I starve you."

"I know, and I love that about you," I sigh. "But if you're going to turn me into a gothic vampire who only drinks blood and things of that nature," I muster, " . . . then let me have one last bite."

I bite into the pumpkin loaf as Axel bites down on my neck. "Axel, wait," I gasp, but my blonde hair turns jet black as he sinks his fangs into me, sexually forcing me to become a vampire. Black angel wings sprout out of my burnt up back. My eyes turn red. I cry blood. We inject the rest of the heroin that hurts. We scream forever because we can never die.

ACKNOWLEDGEMENTS

Thank you

The New York Yankees

The Centre for Expanded Posting

Chica Mob

Miracle Jones

Thomas Sargent Moore

Kat, Paulo, Morg, and Alice

for helping me

BIO

Kathy is an interesting woman from New York.